The Anglo Saxons and Vikings

This book has been designed to bring
Anglo-Saxon and Viking history to life.
The story and pictures provide children
with a useful insight into the period.
However, this is not intended to
be a history text book.

The story and pictures in this book
are all original and have been specially
commissioned for Tesco.

Published for
Tesco Stores Limited
by Brilliant Books Ltd
84-86 Regent Street
London W1R 6DD

First published 1998

Printed by Cambus Litho Ltd, Scotland
Reproduction by Colourpath, England

fun to learn
collection

The Anglo Saxons and Vikings

Edited by *Michael Rosen*

Illustrated by *Andy Hammond*

Alfie hadn't seen his cat for days and decided
to look for him in the old garden shed.
Sure enough, Ginger was asleep under an old box.
While he was rummaging about, he felt a lump in
the pocket of a filthy coat, draped over an old bike.
Alfie started to feel a bit odd and wondered if he was
about to have one of his adventures through time.

He reached inside the coat and pulled out a
dusty brooch, with a few funny bits of coloured
glass in it. He blew on it and – whoa…!
There was that dizzy feeling again, and he
knew he was about to travel back into history…

Alfie found himself in a little
village of thatched huts. It was deserted.
He tiptoed over to one of the huts and peeped
in. There was just one room. In the middle was a
fire with a big pot full of sloppy brown mush, which
smelt utterly disgusting. He was just leaving when he
heard people shouting and cheering in the distance.
Alfie decided to investigate.

He made his way past a pig pen
towards a much larger house with slates
on the roof. "This must belong to the
village chief," Alfie thought.

As he came closer, he saw all the
villagers standing outside. Everyone
was too busy listening and talking to
pay any attention to Alfie.

The chief, who Alfie found out was called a 'thane', was listening to two men who had been fighting. It was a ghastly sight. The thane decided that the rogue, who'd cut off the other man's ear, must pay twenty shillings to his victim and a further eight shillings for knocking out his two front teeth.

Meanwhile, a thief in the crowd was eyeing up Alfie's brooch. And before Alfie realised what had happened, the man had unclipped it and run off. Alfie felt panic grip his throat. Without the brooch, he'd have to stay in this smelly village for ever! He saw the man dart behind a hut. Alfie had no choice – he had to go after him!

The chase took Alfie far from the village, into
some woods and along some cliffs. He could
see that the man had a bad leg and before too
long, he managed to catch up with him.
"Give me back my brooch," demanded Alfie.
"It's mine now, you little brat. I'll get a good
price for this in the next village and you're
not going to stop me!" sneered the thief.

Alfie sat down in
total despair. He was
miserable and wondered
what he was going to do. After a
while, he looked round at the countryside.
It was evening, but he could still see for miles.
There wasn't a house in sight, just rolling hills,
the woods and a deserted beach - far below.

While Alfie looked out to sea, he could just make
out some shapes on the horizon. He waited until he
could see four boats heading towards him. As they
drew closer and closer, Alfie realised
that he'd only ever seen these
boats in books. They were
longships, full of Vikings
ready to raid the
villages nearby!

"I must get back to the village and warn the Anglo Saxons!" thought Alfie.

He turned to have one last look over his shoulder. The Vikings had lit great torches and were already landing on the beach!

By the time Alfie arrived back at the village a feast was in full swing in the thane's hall. There were minstrels playing harps and lyres. And people were drinking mead from cups made from hollowed-out horns. The cups wouldn't stand up, so everyone had to drink down all their mead in one go!

Alfie tried to get their attention, but they were all too drunk to listen. He jumped on to a big table and shouted at the top of his voice. "Vikings! Listen! Er...!"

Most people paid little attention, but the thane told a couple of men to go and see what the boy was talking about.

The men staggered out of the hall still laughing. But no sooner had they turned the corner, than they saw a wave of Viking torches coming straight towards them.

They rushed back into the hall, screaming, "Vikings! Vikings! They'll be here any moment!"

"Run! Run! Save the children, even if the rest of us die!"

VIKINGS!! VIKINGS!!

Alfie scrambled up a nearby tree and watched
the terrifying scene as the Vikings arrived.
They ran into every little hut, grabbed
whatever they could find,
then set it on fire.

The villagers tried to stop them, but the
Vikings, with their long sharp spears and
great big battle-axes, stabbed and crashed
their way through everything.

Alfie could hardly bear to watch. The village was totally destroyed. To his horror, it slowly dawned on him that one of the fires was getting closer and closer to the tree that he was hiding in. Meanwhile, the Vikings were even killing the animals and chasing anyone who was trying to escape. In the distance, he could hear the screams and wails of the women who'd been caught.

Alfie crouched in his tree, unable to move and unable to help. As his eyes blurred over with fear and sadness, he noticed a Viking coming straight towards him. Alfie had been spotted!

Suddenly, one of the villagers ran out from the shadows and attacked the scowling Viking. The Viking forgot all about Alfie and started fighting the brave little villager. Alfie decided that now was the time to make a run for it.

Apart from everything else, he still had to find his brooch!

Alfie ran and ran – through thickets and across open land – until he was certain that he was miles from any Viking. He was just about to collapse from exhaustion, when a great arm gripped his shoulder and lifted him up.

Luckily, it was only an angry Anglo-Saxon farmer, who'd been helping a cow give birth. Alfie was relieved, even though the man smelt like mouldy meat.

"Where have you come from?" said the great oaf.

Alfie tried to tell him about the Viking invasion, but he just grunted and marched off with him under one arm.

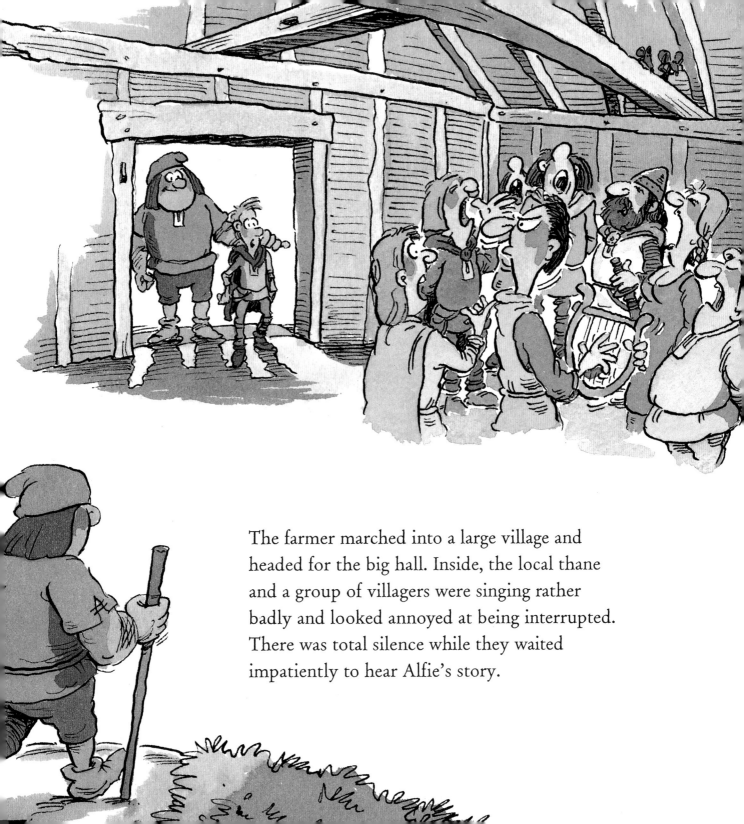

The farmer marched into a large village and headed for the big hall. Inside, the local thane and a group of villagers were singing rather badly and looked annoyed at being interrupted. There was total silence while they waited impatiently to hear Alfie's story.

Alfie poured out his terrible tale of how he'd spotted the Vikings' longships, how they'd marched into the nearby village with their torches and killed most of the people with their great axes. He told them how the bearded invaders had set all the huts on fire and stolen all the villagers' possessions.

The thane and the other men were now listening intently. Their eyes got bigger and bigger. Finally, when Alfie had finished his terrible story, the thane said, "You are a brave lad. You have told us a good story and warned us of dangers that lie ahead for our village. We will have to prepare for dark times and be ready to defend ourselves day and night."

The thane went across the room, opened a wooden casket and reached inside. When he opened his hand, Alfie could not believe his eyes!

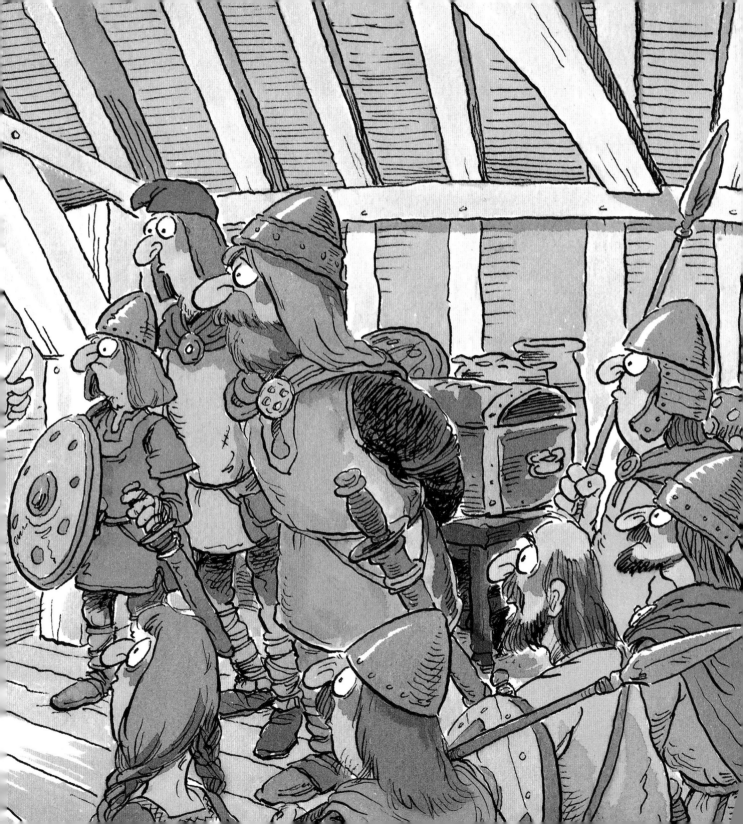

It was his brooch!

"It is our custom to reward a warrior who tells a good story with a brooch," said the thane.

The brooch glinted in the firelight. Alfie thanked him. He was too tired to explain how it had been stolen. He curled up and fell fast asleep. When he woke, he was back in the old shed, still clasping his reward.